# 頑皮一族

Lucy Kincaid 著

Gill Guile 繪

曾蕙蘭 譯

三民書局

Read by Myself     ISBN 1 85854 514 5

Written by Lucy Kincaid and illustrated by Gill Guile

First published in 1996

Under the title Read by Myself

by Brimax Books Limited

4/5 Studlands Park Ind. Estate,

Newmarket, Suffolk, CB8 7AU

# 斑斑學汪汪叫

## Patch Learns to Bark

**P**atch the Puppy lives with his mother, brothers and sisters on **Buttercup** Farm.

Patch can eat his dinner without **spilling** any. He can **wash** behind his ears. But there is one thing Patch cannot do. He cannot bark.

*patch* [pætʃ]
名 斑點

*buttercup* [ˈbʌtəˌkʌp]
名 金鳳花

*spill* [spɪl]
動 灑出

*wash* [waʃ]
動 洗

小狗斑斑跟媽媽和兄弟姊妹住在金鳳花農場裡。
斑斑已經學會自己吃飯，不把飯粒灑出來。斑斑也已經學會怎樣洗自己的耳後根。可是，有一件事情斑斑一直學不會——他不會汪汪叫。

"Do not **worry**," says Mother Dog. "You will learn to bark like the **rest** of us."

The other puppies are not so **kind**. "Patch cannot bark," they **laugh**. "He can only **whimper**!"

*worry* [ˋwɝɪ]
動 擔心

*rest* [rɛst]
名 其他的人

*kind* [kaɪnd]
形 仁慈的

*laugh* [læf]
動 嘲笑

*whimper* [ˋhwɪmpɚ]
動 嗚嗚地哼叫

「別擔心，」狗媽媽說。「你會像我們一樣學會汪汪叫的！」
可是，別的小狗可就沒這麼仁慈了！「斑斑不會汪汪叫，」他們嘲笑著。「他只會嗚嗚地哼叫。」

Patch is so **upset** that he **decides** to **hide** until he has learned how to bark. He does not like his brothers and sisters laughing at him.
He **creeps** over to the barn and sits behind the hay.
There he tries to bark.

*upset* [ʌpˋsɛt]
形 沮喪的

*decide* [dɪˋsaɪd]
動 決定

*hide* [haɪd]
動 躲藏

*creep* [krip]
動 偷偷摸摸地走

斑斑好沮喪喲！他決定躲起來直到學會汪汪叫為止。他不喜歡被他的兄弟姊妹嘲笑。
他悄悄地來到穀倉，坐在乾草堆後面。
他就在那兒練習汪汪叫。

"**G**oodness me!" says Cassie Calf who lives in the barn. "What are you doing there, Patch?"

"I am learning to bark," says Patch **unhappily**.

"I **wish** I could help you," says Cassie.

"I can only **moo**." "**Never mind**," says Patch.

He creeps away to find somewhere else to hide.

*Goodness me!*
天啊！

*unhappily* [ʌnˋhæpɪlɪ]
副 不快樂地

*wish* [wɪʃ]
動 希望

*moo* [mu]
動（牛）哞哞地叫

*Never mind.*
不用擔心，沒什麼

「我的老天啊！」住在穀倉裡的小牛凱西叫道。「你在這兒做什麼啊？斑斑？」

「我在學汪汪叫。」斑斑不快樂地說。

「我真希望能夠幫你。」凱西說。「不過我只會哞哞叫。」

「沒關係！」斑斑說。他悄悄去別的地方躲了起來。

9

**P**atch does not want anyone else to **listen** while he tries to bark. At last he finds a dark **corner** in the hen **run**.

When the chicks **hear** Patch they say to their mother, "Is there a **ghost** in the run?"

"No!" says Mother Hen. "It is only Patch trying to bark."

listen [ˈlɪsn̩]
動 聽

corner [ˈkɔrnɚ]
名 角落

run [rʌn]
名 飼養場

hear [hɪr]
動 聽

ghost [gost]
名 鬼

斑斑不想在練習的時候，被別人聽到。終於，他在雞舍裡找到一個陰暗的角落。小雞們聽到斑斑的聲音，對媽媽說：「雞舍裡是不是有鬼啊？」

「不是啦！」雞媽媽說。「那是斑斑在練習汪汪叫！」

"Can you help him, Mother?" ask the chicks.
"I am afraid not," says Mother Hen. "I can only **cluck**."
Patch **tiptoes** out of the run and goes to the **pig-pen**.

*cluck* [klʌk]
勔 （母雞）咯咯叫

*tiptoe* [ˋtɪpˏto]
勔 用腳尖走

*pig-pen* [ˋpɪgˏpɛn]
名 豬圈

「妳能幫幫他嗎？媽媽？」小雞們問。
「恐怕不行吔！」雞媽媽說。「我只會咯咯叫。」
斑斑躡手躡腳地出了雞舍，往豬圈走去。

When the **piglets** see Patch they all say, "What are you doing in our pig-pen?"

"I am **teaching** myself to bark," says Patch.

"Can we help Patch to bark?" the piglets ask their mother.

"I am afraid not," says Mother Pig.

"We can only **grunt**."

Patch goes to the **stable**.

小豬們看到斑斑，異口同聲地說：
「你在我們的豬圈裡做什麼啊？」
「我在教自己汪汪叫。」斑斑說。
「我們能教斑斑汪汪叫嗎？」小豬們問媽媽。
「恐怕不行呢！」豬媽媽說。「我們只會呼嚕呼嚕叫。」
斑斑去到了馬廄。

"**W**hat can I do for you?" asks Dolly Donkey.

"I am teaching myself to bark," says Patch.

"I would help you if I could," says Dolly, "I can only **bray**. You will find your bark **sooner or later**."

"I have tried very hard and I **still** cannot bark," says Patch.

*bray* [bre]
動 驢叫

*sooner or later*
早晚

*still* [stɪl]
副 仍然

「有什麼我能幫忙的嗎？」驢子桃莉問。

「我在教自己汪汪叫。」斑斑說。

「我真希望能夠幫你呢！」桃莉說，「不過我只會咿呀咿呀叫。你總有一天會學會汪汪叫的。」

「我已經很努力地試過了，我還是不會汪汪叫啊！」斑斑說。

"I have an **idea**," says Dolly. "Why not go and **practice** in the **cellar**? You **might** find your bark there," she says. Patch **leaves** the stable and goes to the cellar. The door is wide open.

「我有一個主意，」桃莉說。「為什麼不去地窖裡練習呢？也許你能在那兒學會汪汪叫喲！」她說。
於是斑斑離開馬廄，往地窖走去。地窖的門敞開著。

Patch goes down the **stairs** very **carefully**. He sees a **chest** lying open at the bottom of the stairs. Patch is very **curious**.

He creeps closer and closer to the chest …

*stair* [stɛr]
名 樓梯

*carefully* [ˈkɛrfəlɪ]
副 小心地

*chest* [tʃɛst]
名 櫃子

*curious* [ˈkjʊrɪəs]
形 好奇的

斑斑小心翼翼地走下樓梯。他看到樓梯底層放著一個開著的櫃子。斑斑很好奇。
他慢慢靠近這個櫃子……

Suddenly a frog **leaps** out and **lands** on Patch's nose!
"**Woof**! Woof!" barks Patch in **surprise**.
"Woof! Woof!" He is so **scared** he runs back up the stairs. He runs all the way home to his mother, barking as he goes.

*leap* [lip]
動 跳

*land* [lænd]
動 掉落

*woof* [wuf]
動 汪叫，低吠

*surprise* [sə`praɪz]
名 驚訝

*scare* [skɛr]
動 使害怕

突然間，一隻青蛙跳了出來，停在斑斑的鼻子上。

「汪！汪！」斑斑嚇得叫了起來。

「汪！汪！」他害怕地跑上樓去，邊跑邊叫地衝回家去找媽媽。

"Woof! Woof!" barks Patch as he **passes** Dolly Donkey in her stable. "Woof! Woof!" barks Patch as he passes the piglets in their pig-pen. "Woof! Woof!" barks Patch as he passes the chicks in their run. "Woof! Woof!" barks Patch as he passes Cassie Calf in her barn.

*pass* [pæs]
動 經過

「汪ㄨㄤ！汪ㄨㄤ！」斑ㄅㄢ斑ㄅㄢ邊ㄅㄧㄢ叫ㄐㄧㄠ，邊ㄅㄧㄢ跑ㄆㄠ過ㄍㄨㄛ在ㄗㄞ馬ㄇㄚ廄ㄐㄧㄡ裡ㄌㄧ的ㄉㄜ驢ㄌㄩ子ㄗ桃ㄊㄠ莉ㄌㄧ。

「汪ㄨㄤ！汪ㄨㄤ！」斑ㄅㄢ斑ㄅㄢ邊ㄅㄧㄢ叫ㄐㄧㄠ，邊ㄅㄧㄢ跑ㄆㄠ過ㄍㄨㄛ在ㄗㄞ豬ㄓㄨ圈ㄐㄩㄢ裡ㄌㄧ的ㄉㄜ小ㄒㄧㄠ豬ㄓㄨ們ㄇㄣ。

「汪ㄨㄤ！汪ㄨㄤ！」斑ㄅㄢ斑ㄅㄢ邊ㄅㄧㄢ叫ㄐㄧㄠ，邊ㄅㄧㄢ跑ㄆㄠ過ㄍㄨㄛ在ㄗㄞ雞ㄐㄧ舍ㄕㄜ裡ㄌㄧ的ㄉㄜ小ㄒㄧㄠ雞ㄐㄧ們ㄇㄣ。

「汪ㄨㄤ！汪ㄨㄤ！」斑ㄅㄢ斑ㄅㄢ邊ㄅㄧㄢ叫ㄐㄧㄠ，邊ㄅㄧㄢ跑ㄆㄠ過ㄍㄨㄛ在ㄗㄞ穀ㄍㄨ倉ㄘㄤ裡ㄌㄧ的ㄉㄜ小ㄒㄧㄠ牛ㄋㄧㄡ凱ㄎㄞ西ㄒㄧ。

"Is that you, Patch?" calls Mother Dog.

"Woof! Woof!" barks Patch.

"I can bark! Something **frightened** me in the cellar and now I can bark!"

Patch's brothers and sisters **crowd** round him.

"I am very **proud** of you, Patch," says Mother Dog. "Woof! Woof!" barks Patch happily.

*frighten* [ˋfraɪtn̩]
勔 驚嚇

*crowd* [kraʊd]
勔 群集

*proud* [praʊd]
形 引以為榮

「那是你嗎？斑斑？」狗媽媽叫喚著。

「汪！汪！」斑斑叫著。

「我會汪汪叫了！在地窖裡有個東西嚇了我一大跳，結果我就會汪汪叫了！」斑斑的兄弟姊妹都擠過來圍著他。

「我以你為榮喲！斑斑。」狗媽媽說。「汪！汪！」斑斑快樂地叫著。

# Say these words again.

| | |
|---|---|
| lives | behind |
| learn | laugh |
| creeps | somewhere |
| hide | anyone |
| corner | trying |
| afraid | teaching |
| sooner | curious |

# Who can you see?

Cassie Calf

Patch

Mother Hen

Dolly Donkey

Mother Dog

# 救難小福星

Heather S Buchanan著　本局編輯部編譯

15×16cm／精裝／6冊

在金鳳花地這個地方，住著六個好朋友：兔子魯波、蝙蝠貝索、老鼠妙莉、
鼴鼠莫力、松鼠史康波、刺蝟韓莉，
他們遇上了什麼麻煩事？要如何解決難題呢？
好多好多精采有趣的歷險記，還有甜蜜溫馨的小插曲，
就讓這六隻可愛的小動物來告訴你吧！

 魯波的超級生日　　 莫力的大災難

 貝索的紅睡襪　　 史康波的披薩

 妙莉的大逃亡　　 韓莉的感冒

老鼠妙莉被困在牛奶瓶了！糟糕的是，她只能在瓶子裡，看著朋友一個個經過卻沒發現她。有誰會來救她呢？

（摘自《妙莉的大逃亡》）

網際網路位址　http://www.sanmin.com.tw

Ⓒ 斑斑學汪汪叫

著作人　Lucy Kincaid
繪圖者　Gill Guile
譯　者　曾蕙蘭
發行人　劉振強
著作財
產權人　三民書局股份有限公司
　　　　臺北市復興北路三八六號
發行所　三民書局股份有限公司
　　　　地址／臺北市復興北路三八六號
　　　　電話／二五〇〇六六〇〇
　　　　郵撥／〇〇〇九九九八——五號
印刷所　三民書局股份有限公司
門市部　復北店／臺北市復興北路三八六號
　　　　重南店／臺北市重慶南路一段六十一號
初　版　中華民國八十八年十一月
編　號　S85536
定　價　新臺幣壹佰玖拾元整
行政院新聞局登記證局版臺業字第〇二〇〇號

有著作權　不准侵害

ISBN　957-14-3089-7（精裝）